# THE

ETHESDA

POEMS

JONATHAN LOVEJOY

*Jonathan Lovejoy*

# THE

# ETHESDA

## POEMS

*Love Beyond the Homeless*

*Jonathan Lovejoy*

Cover: *Reverie On the Edge*, 1893
William Adolphe Bouguereau (1825-1905)

ISBN-10: 0692318844
ISBN-13: 978-0692318843

*For the Homeless*

# Introduction

Jonathan Lovejoy (born Oscar Lee Whitfield, Jr., November 17, 1967) is an American novelist, poet and shortstory writer, whose rejection history makes the author one of the most rejected novelists of all time. His published novels focus heavily on mother-daughter abuse and molestation, often emphasizing generations of violent, abusive mother-daughter relationships. Raised in extreme poverty and domestic abuse, Lovejoy is a graduate of the University of North Carolina at Greensboro (1996) with a B.A. in Religious Studies, and lives in Winston Salem, NC.

Lovejoy is the son of two Pentecostal Holiness preachers from Rocky Mount, NC. On a cold January night in 1992, his father collapsed and was rushed to the hospital, where he died of acute pancreatitis at the age of 46. The strict Pentecostal minister, who had claimed the office of modern day apostle, left behind a wife and ten children.

Written entirely during forty days in a homeless shelter, in March and April 2013 when the author was 45 years old, these four line, simple rhyming verses represent the birth of a completely new poetic style for the author, with terse, old fashioned simplicity of form and execution, evoking the neo-rhyming spirit of Longfellow, while looking forward in content toward the end of this age of human history. Ranging in topic from homelessness to the Second Coming of Christ, these unique, peculiar poems are an expression of the author's profound grief and confusion, while living amongst the most disillusioned and forgotten people in this land of latter day prosperity, where sometimes, hopelessness is their daily bread, and the wine of despair is the only nourishment for a weary soul.

*Jonathan Lovejoy*

# THE

## POEMS

or

# "Love Beyond the Homeless"

*Jonathan Lovejoy*

*Such is the grandest music among us—*

*Poets...*

*Such are the wildest thoughts among us—*

*Composers...*

# Love Beyond the Homeless

# I

*March 17th to March 23rd*

*Jonathan Lovejoy*

# 1

Swirl precious harmonies in righteous pearl

Where the spirit of the Lord doth rule the world

Comet sensibilities will give this a whirl

As the eve of the Second Coming of Christ unfurls

# 2

Hellbound souls adrift in the wind

Back and forth and then back again

Never understanding all the trouble that they're in

'Til God judges them in the Lake of Fire because of sin

3

Out here in the world, in the cold

Establish a rock of faith in me

That you and I may come together, O Lord—

And deliver the Promise that is meant to be

# 4

*R*eestablish thy walk of faith in me

O Heavenly Father, that I may obtain thy favor

With you and I as friends in Heaven and Earth

In a future of joy and happiness to savor

*I* am supposed to picture an estate

Amherst at St. Carmen in the Fields

An end of the world sign of his coming

With righteousness and faith as my sword and shield

Establish thy blessing with me, O Lord

That it may not be lost from me again

Remove the Devil's haunted touch from my skin

And this place of poverty I've been hiding in

# 7

Trial and error is where you learn

In your walk with God

It is the fire in which we burn

This desire to walk where angels trod

A Shakespearean whale swims the night sea
In the awe and splendor of majesty
Never ending grandeur and effortless ability
To dominate and rule in power and epic divinity

## 9

The spirit of Christ is the spirit of poetry

When Love and devotion are the key

This emotion of divine sensibility—

Seeks to flourish the world in epic gentility

# 10

Please God, have mercy on me

Restore my life to what it used to be

Save me from the Devil's prophecy

Help me have joy and prosperity

# 11

*T*his is your special eating pattern

Yours and yours alone

To allow your body two days to recover

From feasting down to the marrow of bone

# *12*

The life of a homeless person is a lonely place to be
Through the library and bus station windows to see
Looking for the power of the mighty hand of God—
To restore a life in Love's Humility

# *13*

*L*eap across the gulf to the other side of life
Where the mighty hand of God hath carried you through
Only a miracle can save you from you
Until the mercy of God restores your life anew

# 14

Except the decision that God hath made

To devastate your life and put you in the shade

But expect a miracle for the plan he hath laid

To restore you and your wife after the price has been paid

# 15

Lost, lonely souls in an elevator

Riding up and down to nowhere

Unable to hope, unable to care

Whether judgment or destiny hath put them there

# *16*

I tried to push my helpmate away
To the devastation of my immortal soul
Until the gun manifested in my dreams—
To kill the idea that the marriage is old

# 17

The truth of how the love of my life must feel

Is devastation by the punishment of God revealed

Until his mercy doth have this chastisement repealed

So we can take hands and walk the twilight harvest field

Father, forgive us for the sins we know

For the paradise we devastated with a disobedient heart

Let love be our final resting place to go—

With only peacefulness and Love's Humility to regard

# *19*

O Heavenly Father, in the mighty name of Jesus
I have a favor to ask of thee
Send your protection to this unworthy soul—
From the arrival of apocalyptic misery

# 20

The Lord rode me on a bus to somewhere
With joy and happiness in my soul to bear
Though the Devil hath destroyed all in life that I love—
My end-of-the-world calling from God is still there

# *21*

*T*he sounds and lights of earthy progression
Flashing red through the streets of predawn derision
Screaming hopelessness and fear to every lonely soul adrift—
To help or hinder them in their lifeline decision

# 22

Heavenly Father, rescue me from this Hell I'm in
These unbelievable consequences of disobedience and sin
Kept across a great gulf from the woman that I love—
Waiting for thy tender mercies descended like a dove

# 23

Have faith in God and you will see

The full restoration of your family

Where love will rule in tranquility—

With the spirit of Christ in humility

# 24

He sent me an umbrella in the pouring rain
To protect me from the icy deluge of suffering and pain
God is trying to tell me that there is nothing more to gain—
Doubt and unbelief have no further use in this domain

# 25

The music of their snoring
Was enough to keep me occupied
When I checked into a homeless shelter
And lost every ounce of my pride

# 26

Stay on the bus until the rhyme of night

Stay on the bus until the evening night

Let the Holy Spirit be your ride into the night

Get the Holy angels to be your a guide to what is right

# 27

*H*ere's one more fact that's good to know

A demon took the lost colony where they didn't want to go

The word "CROW-AH-TOW-AHN" was painted over the gates of Hell

Because the spirit of Sodom and Gommorah descended in ways too deep to tell

*Jonathan Lovejoy*

# II

*March 24<sup>th</sup> to March 30<sup>th</sup>*

Lord, bless me to breathe free

Keep shortness of breath at bay

Until I can go home with my wife again—

And love her in the evening day

# 29

*I* rebuke you Satan, in Jesus' name

Wherever it is that you are

For God hath not given me the spirit of fear

But has left my favorite cookies in a jar

# 30

To be abandoned by the woman that you love

Is more somber than the death of a mourning dove

Left to fend for yourself in the cold

While wishing you had the love of your life to hold

# *31*

Avoid negativity and you will see
Uncompromising positivity
The perfect life that's meant to be
Is yours by the Holy Trinity

# 32

*W*ake up with positivity and you will see

A life of perfect peace and prosperity

A ride in comfort and heavenly beauty

Bestowed by God as his solemn duty

# 33

Satan is done

Though he thinks he's only just begun

God is preparing you for a perfect ride

Of peace and prosperity and a restoration of your pride

# *34*

*B*the mercy and grace of God you are in like Flynn

An earthly term to describe the peace and prosperity you're in

Earthly wealth and riches and the favor of women and men—

Because you chose to delight yourself in the Lord again and again and again

et others be as negative as what they want to be

It is your job to foster love and positivity

The spirit of Christ is the spirit of Love is the way its going to be

Now let the music of the world around you lull you to a perfect rest and sleep

# 36

Leave doubt and unbelief behind
Uncompromising faith is the key
To rise above the Devil's influence
From here to eternity

# 37

Uncompromising obedience is the key
To a future of joy and prosperity
Praise the Lord and watch and see—
Him rescue you from trash and poverty

*T*he Holy Ghost is teaching you humility

Be it the midst of suffering or sin

Keep your mouth shut and watch the power of God move

To get you out of the trouble you're in

# *39*

God will repair a broken marriage

Despite all transgression and sin

To create Love's humility like he said he would

Time and time again

# 40

Navigate the sleepy waters of discontent

Arise from thy slumber to go where you are sent

Set sail in the wind of the sunrisen sea

To find the shores of your destiny

# 41

Keep your mouth shut and you will see

The power of God move magically

A perfect life is your destiny

From here to the shores of eternity

# 42

Infuse myself with thee, O Lord
With thine vulnerability and humility
And that imbued by the power of God—
With love and the twilight mountain's majesty

# 43

*I* love thee to die for thee, o Lord

Despite what perfect life you may have for me

Bathe me in thy peculiar sweetness, my Savior

In the power of thine epic Humility

*Jonathan Lovejoy*

# III

*March 31$^{st}$ to April 6$^{th}$*

# 44

*B*e positive and shake the dust off your feet

And see that the power of God cannot be beat

The Devil has already been crushed to defeat

Despite their efforts to put you on the street

# 45

A profound evil has been abated

According to all the promises he made

Now pack your bags and go home to your wife

To rest and recover in the evening day

# 46

*I*f you keep your mouth shut then you will see

The power of God move magically

Devote your life to him diligently

And watch him save you expediently

# 47

A reprobate mind cannot be changed

Except by the perfect will of God

When the love of Christ no longer remains

And Christ-like behavior is deemed curious and odd

*F*rom here to the end of your perfect life

Fret not what happened to you and your wife

Because the promise of God is uncontained

As what monumental blessings bestowed doth sill remain

# 49

The beauty of a marriage broken and repaired
Is in the ugliness of God's wrath and devastation
Like the freedom tower out of the rubble of nine eleven—
Reaching from the ground up to the shores of Heaven

# 50

The other side of judgment is God's mercy

Restoration and reward

A time for healing and reconciliation

And recovery from the Devil's wicked sword

# *51*

*Y*ou're going to have a perfect life
Your faith will be restored
I promise, saith the spirit of God
I promise, saith the Lord

# 52

*A* bus station is a nightmare of hopelessness
The accursed—drifting to and fro
Victims of destiny, cold and bleak
Spirits with nowhere left to go

The sad remains to human bones unperturbed

Is the Wicked Witch of the East who divorced her husband undisturbed

Even though her feelings toward him were undeserved

When God had mercy and reconciled their marriage undeterred

*Jonathan Lovejoy*

# IV

*April 7ᵗʰ to  to April 13ᵗʰ*

# 54

Divine assurance of billionaire status

That I may ride the bus in tranquility

So I don't have to be afraid all the time

While I wait for Love's Humility

Rest in the Lord and wait patiently

He will restore thine whole life unto thee

Where the past is a distant and bygone memory

In a home of Love and Tranquility

$\mathcal{I}$wish you so much joy and happiness

This saith the Lord God of hosts

Where there is no longer a reason to fear—

A life filled with pain and forgotten ghosts

*A*crossing over into a new life

Absent from the pain of bitterness and strife

Waiting for restoration to the woman who was my wife

To a time where there are no bitter words that cut like a carving knife

Living with Aurora was like living in Hell

An evil and wishy washy witch's spell

Charity and goodwill on the surface did her well

To hide a soul of sadism and demonic wickedness to tell

*R*iding the bus in tranquility

Waiting for my heart of soulmate civility

To pick up where we left off in anointed ability

And warm each other's hearts in Love's Humility

The number 18 and the number 43

Were the beginning and the end of my poverty

When God told me to abandon hopelessness

And ride 18 and 43 to prosperity

If you choose not to eat

You choose to stay thin

A bank of calories that for the first time in your life

Is set up so that you can win

When you cast your cares at the foot of the cross

In the sunrise of a beautiful day

God will restore your marriage and your writing

In an unknown, unseen and impossible way

Have joy and happiness saith the Lord
And you'll defeat the Devil's wicked sword
With strength and power to live your perfect life
The one he promised was your just reward

# 64

*R*ide the bus in tranquility
And wait for Love's Humility
Until he decides to restore your life
With anointed ability

# 65

The life you've been promised is yours

Have faith until the eagle soars

It does not matter how many blackbirds the Devil brings

Wait and see what the dove has in store

66

Wake up the spirit of Christ in your life

To protect you from demons of hopelessness and strife

Now walk the perfect path he has guided you in

Until your destiny manifests your wife and your mansion within

Infuse me with this profound belief
*"A billionaire from my writing"* will save me from grief
With the wife of my dreams at my heart to stay—
On the balcony of our mansion in the evening day

*T*he blessings of God are absolute

Given without compromise and no rebuke

The promise of God is fashioned and fitted like a brand new suit

Wear it with Faith and confidence that the blessing and Almighty power of God is yours to boot

*V*ent the negativity and let it go

Deep in private where the ugliness won't show

Then repent and move on from the the thought crimes you've laid

Content that no evil path toward another person was laid

Embrace the spirit of positivity

Leave negativity behind

Ad watch God give you a perfect life

Better than the one you have in mind

# 71

To become a billionaire from your writing

Is still yours to achieve

Bestowed by the spirit of God

Who hath blessed the impossible to believe

# 72

If you choose to eat you'll be fat overnight
Because you have such a large and gross appetite
Monitor your eating and guard it with your life—
So God can give you your heart's delight

# 73

Please help me this morning, O precious Lord

Happiness to achieve

That I may live an abundant life

With no further causes left to grieve

# 74

My love for thee is infinity, O Lord
The life and death of me
My desperation is for thee, O Lord
The life and breath of me

# 75

Holy Ghost—come to me

Comfort me with truth and tranquility

The greatest novelist of all time—

And my wife in Love's Humility

# 76

The morning day is dawn's early light

Nearby the edge of night

Shadows recall fair birth of light

Beyond their feeble sight

# 77

You'll see your dove at the end of the day
Or somewhere along the way
To reestablish your end of the world calling from God—
And her sweetness restored in the Evening Day

*Jonathan Lovejoy*

# V

*April 14ᵗʰ to April 20ᵗʰ*

The power of God is your reality

To bless you and keep you and sustain your mentality

Despite every negative thing you see

God will move to protect your tranquility

# 79

Obey the Almighty God and you will see

Your life come together magically

Things will happen that you won't believe

Impossible for others to achieve

The period at the end of the sentence is the dove

To help restore your marriage to a place of love

By the mercy and power of the Almighty God

Love's Humility is what I'm dreaming of

# 81

*I* would like to feed the people this magic

These books that I've been hiding in

So that I may live the abundant life

God promised that I would be riding in

The music of their snoring is a nuisance beyond repair

Homeless shelter noises—

Sending Hellish sounds into the air

As I endeavor to sleep to keep from crumbling underneath despair

*I* saw the white dove on faith in my marriage

To give a dark spirit life and hope

That someday we'll be together again—

Despite sins and trespasses too deep to know

Oh Lord, infuse me with what it is I need

So I can endeavor to be the best indeed

With no pretense nor tendency for greed

But merely the fulfillment of Fate and Destiny harvested from the seed

Infuse me with joy and happiness, o Lord

That I may serve and walk with thee

Overflow my heart with gladness, O Lord

That my calling might manifest tonight in me

# 86

Take the opportunity to eat where its at
Or you'll wind up starving like a hungry stray cat
Some meals God'll provide cannot make you fat
But be thankful that he fed you—and that is that

*T*ake care of the mourning dove

For the reconciliation you've been dreaming of

Let the power of God show you the way

To have your wife again in the Evening Day

*V*ictory is mine saith the Lord

Over the Devil and his wicked sword

O'er the profound evil that was done to thee

That was done with such heartlessness and sadistic glee

$\mathcal{Y}$ou have to be happy to get ready to be sad

Its called "hopeful melancholy"

Life sucks and you move on

So you can endure the Devil's folly

# 90

Love as the gentle rose in spring

Is a profoundly blessed thing

A gift bestowed by the Almighty God

Flowed upon the dove's blue and sounding melancholy wing

# *91*

Hope and renewal in the rising sun

A circle of orange and crimson light

Burnt amber about the trees of life

On the eve of the Second Coming of Christ

# 92

Obey the Almighty God and you will see

Your life come together magically

Things will happen that you won't believe

Impossible for others to achieve

# 93

Our nearest and sweet blessing

Is on the Walmart floor for you

Do your job and do it well

So you'll have a good billionaire's story to tell

# 94

You come across as a disciple of Christ
With a shining mansion upon a hill
Cursed to walk the streets in a lonely life
Until the mercy of Christ moves upon his will

# 95

Ride the bus to a perfect life

From here to the reconciliation with your wife

Where all will be restored without bitterness and strife

On our walk with the Lord by the mind of Christ

# 96

Commune with the Lord

And he'll commune with you

He'll give you the life you've always wanted

Its easy for Him to do

# VI

*April 21ˢᵗ to April 25ᵗʰ*

# 97

A dark cloud of trouble being lifted away

Cut like the branches of a dead tree sway

Watch magical ability come back to stay

By the mercy and power of God today

98

Obedience to God is the key

To a life filled with magic and prosperity

To avoid all the Devil's witchery

And rest in the promise of God's love and integrity

# 99

Wait on the Lord so you can see

The power of God move mightily

A transforming fabric to display God's love and beauty

In Joy, happiness and prosperity

# *100*

Obedience to God is still the key

To a life filled with magic and prosperity

Watch im do things other people won't see

As you come to know him intimately

# *101*

Rest at the throne of Almighty God

After the trauma you've been through

By way of the cross of Jesus Christ

And the power of the Holy Spirit that lives in you

# 102

Keep your mouth shut and live the power of God
And let the Holy Spirit guide you
He'll lead you to places high and low
From skid row to the mansion where he'll hide you

# *103*

*T*he black cat was one last and final sign unto you

That its time for you to have faith and push the barrier through

The power of God in your life has an Armageddon view

That the end of the world and the Second Coming of Jesus Christ is overdue

# 104

The greatest novelist of all time
Was yours before you went to bed
Now it's yours for the rest of your life
There's nothing more left to be said

# ABOUT THE AUTHOR

Jonathan Lovejoy is a graduate of the University of North Carolina at Greensboro, with a B.A. in Religious Studies. He currently lives in Winston Salem, North Carolina.

For more info on the author's life and career, visit jonathanlovejoy.com